Reality Reframed

A Short Collection of Mystical Science Fiction

Reality Reframed

A Short Collection of Mystical Science Fiction

EDWARD N BROWN

CRYSTAL SEA PRESS
CHICAGO, ILLINOIS

REALITY REFRAMED
A Short Collection of Mystical Science Fiction

Copyright © 2024 by Edward N Brown

Scripture quotations in this work are taken from:
The New American Bible, Revised Edition, Copyright © 2010, 1991, 1986, by the Confraternity of Christian Doctrine, Washington, DC, and are used by permission of the copyright owner. All Rights Reserved. No part of the New American Bible may be reproduced in any form without permission in writing from the copyright owner.
The New Revised Standard Version Bible: Catholic Edition, Copyright © 1993 and 1989 by the Division of Christian Education of the National Council of the Churches of Christ in the USA. Used by permission. All rights reserved. No part of the New Revised Standard Version Bible may be reproduced in any form without permission in writing from the copyright owner.

ISBN: 979-8-9884089-5-6

Published by Crystal Sea Press
Chicago, IL
Printed in the United States of America
CSP
For information about this title, or to order other books and/or electronic media, contact the publisher at: http://www.crystalseapress.com

CONTENTS

INTRODUCTION

This booklet falls under the classifying genre of 'Biblical Speculative Fiction' or 'Christian Science Fiction'.

According to Wikipedia, 'Biblical Speculative Fiction' is speculative fiction that uses Christian themes and incorporates the Christian worldview. Alternatively, 'Christian Science Fiction is a subgenre of both Christian literature and science fiction, in which there are strong Christian themes, or Christian point of view.

In actuality, the stories in this booklet are simply entertaining and thought-provoking tales based on science, but with a mild biblical or Christian reference view. However, the science is not 'hard' and the reference view is not 'strong'.

In any case, trying to define science fiction is a vague and imprecise task. The author agrees with the well-known saying that "the Bible is not science fiction and science fiction is not the Bible."

The stories herein simply fill the public appetite for anything about imagination — anything that is far away from the drudge of reality. It's entertainment mostly, but still within the general worldview values of mainstream Christian society.

Three stories fall under the rubric of alien encounters. But the takeaway from each story may be different for each and every reader.

The first story, **Reframing the Non-Interference Directive,** presents a spinoff of the political/philosophical principle popularized in the "Star Trek" series of TV shows – that we should not interfere with the development of other-worldly cultures and societies. However, in this story, many different diplomatic approaches (some interfering and some not) are tried, and all are found wanting in one way or another. Over time, the diplomatic process winds its way to a final logical conclusion.

The second story, **Dimensional Waves, Energy Transmission, and Magical Information Transfer,** is a straightforward account (the curious title notwithstanding) of an alien culture whose instincts for exploration pushes them to the very edges of science and religion. How much like them are we? And what is the most likely scenario for a future when at the very extremes? Furthermore, how will a breakdown, glitch, or anomaly affect the possible futures?

The third story, **The World of the Emissaries**, is a strange tale of periodic alien visitation over the millennia. At first just 'Watchers' but then teachers and helpers, the whole alien encounter experience unravels into an ugly mess of immorality, violence, and conundrum. Evil giants roam the land and human civilization is threatened. The aliens try to correct the degraded evolution by use of an extermination event. But there are survivors – and they slowly begin to turn evil again. What will the alien visitors do now?

As a bonus, a more lighthearted tale is included as a fourth story. Not involving alien encounters, it is more a mythological exercise than science fiction. Based on folk legend, **Andrei and the Beautiful Vampiress** is a compelling story with moral overtones and subtle insights. It's a story with real heroes and villains set in a fairytale atmosphere, and with a fairytale ending. But like a good story, there are a few twists and turns along the way — especially at the end.

1 – REFRAMING THE NON-INTERFERENCE DIRECTIVE

<fade-in with stylish music>

"Good evening, ladies and gentlemen, this eighth of September 2315 – and welcome to **Interglobal Insights** – the award-winning weekly news-magazine that gives you crucial information regarding the policies and events of our world's complex interactions with other intelligent cultures and societies in the galaxy. I'm Walter Townsend.

"With us tonight is Dr. Robert Nelmec, director of the Institute of Interplanetary Relations, and foremost authority on foreign cultures.

"Dr. Nelmec, welcome to the show."

"Thank you very much – always a pleasure to be here."

"So, given recent disturbances on a number of worlds, demonstrations against human presence and influence, and the looming threats of violence and repositioning, the topic that seems to be on everyone's mind this week is how best to interact with foreign cultures – such that peace and tranquility is maintained while our strategic and economic interests are assured.

"What is your take on the current situation?"

"Well, first let me say that relations with otherworldly cultures is extremely difficult. Cultural differences can be enormous – remember, each society has independently evolved for thousands, or tens-of-thousands, of years. There are bound to be glitches and bumps-in-the-road. That being said, I must remind everyone that we have made tremendous progress since the dark ages of yesteryear, the repercussions of which we are still struggling with today.

"But let me digress for a bit, and recap what has been done in the past:

The Report

"Once Upon a Time we had a foreign policy tenet called the **Non-interference Directive**. It pertained to space exploration and the discovery of new worlds, new life forms, and new civilizations. We were actually proud of it at the time. But after a few centuries, like many laws and statutes enacted by bureaucrats and politicians even with the best intentions, it was found to be wanting. The original thinking was that this approach of not interfering in the internal affairs of another sovereign society would result in less foreign contamination – a healthier natural growth and evolution of intelligent sentient beings in a nascent civilization.

"But this was found not to be the case. The simple knowledge of an alien culture would undoubtedly affect the evolution of the society. Even without any advice, suggestions, or indirect help of any kind (and I'm obligated to say here that even with the best intentions, social interference of some kind often occurred, especially in humanitarian or rescue situations), the society altered its natural evolution in strange and unpredictable ways. The foreign contact and knowledge of the existence of aliens, was enough to vastly change the landscape of the society. And invariably, conflicts and squabbles arose between the alien newcomers and the indigenous natives. These could get ugly and just create further ongoing problems that never seemed to resolve.

"Now, it's understandable that this non-interference approach might be preferable to the earlier more direct approaches used in the global exploration of earth, where the desire for resources was paramount and the concern for individual welfare was relegated to spiritual education (which was difficult because of the enormous gap in personal worldviews). The early result was usually death from disease or war, or cultural destruction. Even the later follow-on approach of 'live-and-let-live', or 'peaceful coexistence' didn't fare much better. There was always acrimony, bitterness, and constant altercations between the native and foreign peoples.

"But once in the arena of space, with the possibility for contact with new societies and cultures, the necessity for implementing the right protocols for contact and interaction became absolutely mandatory. Things couldn't be done as they were done before. New policies had to be formulated. And so, they were. The 'Non-interference Directive' was one of the first, but lasted only a short time. Glitches and blips in the policy made it apparent that other approaches were needed."

"A succeeding policy was the strategy known as **Clandestine Watching**. Under this directive, the foreign society was watched secretly behind invisible barriers – the people had no idea they were being observed and monitored. There was no personal contact. This yielded a great deal of third-party humdrum information but little insight into the formative aspects of the society. And the technology, processes, and equipment required was very expensive. Furthermore, in almost all of the societies surveilled, the result was always the same. The society either stagnated – never progressing in culture or enlightenment – or it fractionated into multiple small divisions, each believing in its own superiority and constantly at war with its neighbors. What little advancement did occur was always driven by war (or the threat of war) and oriented toward the elevation and retention of power and status of the elite. We really wanted the cultures to progress, but they just didn't. It was frustrating."

"Later, this policy was modified to become the strategy called **Undercover Infiltration**, popularly understood as the policy where a plant, mole, or spy was sent in to secretly mix among the people and become 'one of them'. Many such spies were utilized. This person would look and act just like a native, but would gather information on the formative processes of the society. Of course, it was very difficult to surgically modify an individual and even more difficult to train them how to act and speak like a native. Invariably, problems arose – the surgical appearance would break down (resulting in awkward fix-ups), situations would arise where the agent was unprepared (and could appear strange or suspicious), accidents could expose the agent to unwanted physical examinations (which would require a 'cover-up' to be implemented), and even occurrences where the agents became psychologically disoriented (being overly immersed in the foreign culture).

To gather useful information over the long term, many undercover infiltrators were required, widely dispersed throughout the society. And as a natural consequence, the number of problems requiring some kind of intervention became immense. Eventually, the policy became unwieldly, and it was slowly abandoned in favor of other approaches. Attempts to extract the infiltrators without causing local suspicion became a continuing complicated headache. Even to this day, it is thought that a handful of undercover infiltrators could still exist on a number of alien worlds – official records could never close the books on every agent dispersed into the field. This, of course, fueled a lot of speculation about possible inter-species procreation, and all sorts of affiliated chatter – a ripe stockpile for sensationalist stories, which are still popular today."

"Consequently, the leaders of our civilized world came up with a new and innovative policy. They called it **Assisted Principled Guidance**. It was hoped that this policy would eliminate or circumvent the ills and misfortunes of the earlier direct approaches, yet still accomplish something worthwhile, which the non-interference approaches weren't. The goal was not just to learn, but to mold, or shape, the indigenous behavior so as to be more consistent with the desired behavior of an advanced enlightened society – and to do this in a manner totally imperceptible to the target entity (be it individual, group, or society). The foreign guidance would be gradual, unnoticeable, and undetectable. The foreigners would literally 'get inside the heads' of the natives. And they would teach them, guide them, and convince them that certain behaviors were better than others (policy detractors always claimed that it was just brainwashing by another name).

"The policy was implemented under the guise of visitors, or foreigners, who blended into the fabric of society at all horizontal and vertical echelons. The visitors were from some hypothetical faraway land, culture, or society, who just happened to arrive in the targeted place by accident or misfortune. But they brought with them their skills, knowledge, processes, hopes, and desires, that they willfully espoused on the natives (some say it was literally forced on them) under the rubric of 'helping out' or 'making it better'.

"The policy did have some 'high points', but again there were problems. A huge amount of training was required for a 'visitor', with constant updating and control of 'situational awareness' by the central command back home. Inevitably, there were difficulties and complications. Foreigners were often resented or marginalized. "What do they know anyway?", "Who do they think they are?", and "They think they're better than us" (the 'not-one-of-us syndrome') were common sayings among the natives. And there was always suspicions about where they came from and why they were here, leading to conspiracy theories and third-column invasion apprehensions."

"It was realized that a new policy was needed, but it wasn't until we had developed new technology, that we had the courage to implement it universally. Facilitated and energized by technology that allowed for the copying of both memory and processing patterns (data and programs) from the storage memory of a master computer (using the latest bio-cell or gel-pack memory systems) into the minds of individual people, without any conscious realization by the recipient, the policy was introduced with great fanfare.

"The donor patterns were from the brightest and most highly trained minds in the civilized world, integrated together, and saved into the massive bio-memory stores of the largest supercomputers – a true knowledge bank. They were then copied and uploaded surreptitiously into the minds of the most powerful and influential native leaders. The targeted individual was clandestinely abducted under general anesthesia and brought to a secret lab facility, where he underwent the upload procedure (he received a download), and then released back into society, totally unaware of any interference. And sure enough, the native recipients behaved just like the civilized donors would behave in all the day-to-day situations encountered. In this manner, the policy of **Immersive Principled Guidance** was triumphantly implemented in many societies on many worlds."

"But there was a long-term problem. Despite all the laws, rules, regulations, and enforcement procedures enacted by the government to enable social correctness (and which work pretty well in our earthly culture), and incorporated into the software of the master supercomputer knowledge-base, tiny blips, nuances, and glitches in the coded software interface into the human psyche often resulted in suboptimal performance. Eventually, deep innate human drives would always surface to the top, superseding the implanted rules and laws. The person's deepest instincts would override all other programmed knowledge and reasoning, and his behavior would degrade to instinctual behavior.

"It was a predictable behavior but it was random. We knew what the identified proxy carrier person would probably do, but we never knew exactly when he would do it. We tried to refine and upgrade the software for many years, but we could never control, much less eliminate, the instinctual behavior. There were continuing isolated, but serious, problems."

"So that brings us up to today. Many mainstream government, industry, and academic scholars now believe that the only workable and economically feasible solution is **Remote Surveillance**. Akin to 'Clandestine Watching', the world's culture and societies are secretly monitored – but in this case, it is from deep space. No invisible shields or hidden monitoring alcoves, the process is stealthy but much more economical. Only a few cloaked satellites filled with remote sensing and telemetry equipment are needed – no personnel on away-missions to get mixed up in local affairs. Of course, the quantity, quality, and specificity of data returned is much less robust. But hey – the thinking is that since most worlds don't progress toward a civilization the way we would like it to, in any case, why bother trying to force it or shape it to our model? Just a cursory noncomprehensive observation of many worlds over the long term could reveal the deserving exception that IS visitable with a well-planned 'First Contact'. Cheaper, less problems, and the potential remains for possible contact and relations."

"But it must be pointed out that there is a sizable minority of scholars, often backed by vociferous students, political activists, and media affiliates, who insist that all cultures and societies in the galaxy should be actively steered into conforming with a set of predefined laws, rules, regulations, and procedures (called social engineering in past years), that they believe are based on altruism, equality, personal rights, and social cohesion, Somewhat like our own culture in operation, but they dare to seek even further changes and incorporate them into the master social knowledge bank software – greater memory and increased program sophistication for enhanced uploads into the minds of more and more individuals.. It's simply known as **Total Immersion Guidance**. They advocate direct interference of all kinds into foreign cultures, so long as it furthers the overarching goals – and they are willing to take the bumps and bruises along the way because they believe that their cause is noble. 'The good of the many overrides the suffering of the few' is their motto. Of course, there is always the possibility that something goes drastically wrong and a catastrophe occurs, but that possibility is downplayed as being so improbable that it's almost impossible.

"Now, there is a movement afoot that has been widely promoted in the media, to begin an experimental program on a remotely isolated region of a designated planet, whereby large quantities of individuals would be selected for surreptitious uploading of the enhanced social knowledge base. Now, this is considered as a scientific experiment, confined to one region of one planet. And it will take years or decades to evaluate the results. But it seems to be a sort of compromise on the issue of interplanetary relations.

"So, that's where we stand right now."

The Commentary

"Thank you very much Dr. Nelmec. And now, to provide some commentary on this topic, we have with us Mr. Tony Rinsdorf, a respected analyst with the Peace and Liberty foundation, a reputable think-tank on global and inter-global affairs. Good evening Mr. Rinsdorf, and welcome to the show."

"Good evening and thanks for having me."

"It's become apparent over the last few weeks, that there exists some strong criticism of this latest compromise on the 'Immersion Guidance' policy of interplanetary relations. There have been some harsh editorials and even some protest demonstrations. Can you enlighten us as to what exactly are the issues here?"

"Yes, I'd be happy to. There is a growing concern among many citizens that the technique of immersive guidance, or total immersion guidance in the extreme, goes too far. It impinges upon the basic liberty of the individual."

"But those concerns have been raised for years now, Mr. Rinsdorf, and the general consensus is that it's OK if it leads to a more peaceful, benevolent, and harmonious society. What's changed? Just the complexity and sophistication of the knowledge base?"

"It's more than that," Mr. Townsend. "The real fear is that this technique of secretly uploading a social knowledge base into the mind of an individual may be used on citizens of earth. And that would amount to a grievous invasion of privacy. Doing strange things to individuals on a strange planet many light-years away is one thing – not too many people pay attention. But doing it to your own kind on your own world is quite another thing – it makes many people sit up and take notice."

"But Mr. Rinsdorf, isn't that a bit paranoid? There really isn't any evidence that such a thing could or would ever happen."

"But that's where you're wrong. There is a new socio-political movement here on earth that is growing in strength every day. They are radicals who go beyond the folks who insist that all cultures and societies in the galaxy should be actively steered into conforming with a set of our predefined social laws. These activists want to implement that policy here on earth – a 'group-think' by any other name! In fact, they want to do it now with full speed ahead. You see, they're tired of the same old shallow words and acts that have been bandied about for hundreds of years. They want real change and they want it now! And they don't care how they get it."

"So, what evidence do you have? Do you have specifics?"

The Expose and Denunciation

"Yes, I do, and that's why I'm here. I have evidence that this group of radicals has friends, advocates, and collaborators at all levels of government, industry, and academia. It's not just a bunch of long-haired hippies, it's a new and organized movement, orchestrated by big, powerful, and influential guys at the highest levels.

"In fact, I can announce today that there are top-secret 'black programs' deep within the CIA and other government agencies working right now to develop and covertly disperse a social knowledge base into the minds of individuals here on earth. And this is not just for criminals, the mentally unstable, or the mentally disadvantaged – but is meant for all people, especially those targeted by these programs for political, economic, or religious reasons.

"Now listen, I believe that over 100 volunteer subjects have already received the social knowledge base installation by a hard-wired download in a clandestine computer lab somewhere – and it has been executed and run successfully. And these subjects may be totally unaware that their minds have been altered. So, why did they do it, you may ask? For whatever reason – social brainwashing, political indoctrination, behavioral conditioning – they actually believed that it was the noble thing to do – for society, the world, and the galaxy. And how many coerced subjects were forced to receive the social knowledge base installation is anybody's guess.

"Of course, I can't name names of either subjects, administrators, or managers. That would just bring denials, lawsuits, diversions, and strategy shifts.

"But that's not the worst of it. If it was, this would just be another investigative watchdog report. In reality, I have discovered a conspiracy at the highest levels – a conspiracy meant to change the lives of millions of people, as well as the fabric of our society. You see, the social knowledge base isn't restricted to being uploaded or downloaded over wires in a lab – it can be transmitted over the existing wireless networks and readily disseminated globally. You've noticed those new weather stations and telescopes being installed on nearby mountain-tops? How about all those upgrades to the cell-phone towers? Ever wonder what exactly is being installed?

"Well, I'm telling you now that hidden deep within the standard operating functionality is covert technology that enables the transmission of the social knowledge base on a carrier wave that is finely tuned to the specific frequencies of the brain's parietal lobes – allowing for signals to be directly input to the thalamus and the amygdala without first being processed by sensory neurons in the spinal cord and the peripheral nervous system. It's like injecting the information directly into the cerebrum. This technology is made possible by research that uncovered the basic receiver-like attributes of the parietal lobes (receptivity, sensitivity, and discrimination). In other words, they've found the receiving antenna in the brain.

"It's being implemented now – and not just as a limited experimental application. It's a full-fledged deployment. And it's not limited to weather stations, telescopes, and cell-phone towers. Look at all the commercial airplanes flying overhead. In the belly of each fuselage is a social knowledge base transmitter. Do you sense anything different when a plane flies overhead?"

The Denial and Deflection

"Now Mr. Rinsdorf, this is all a bit much. Surely, if such a covert conspiracy was occurring, someone would be aware of it and sound the alarm. It can't have gotten very far."

"If you really believe that, Mr. Townsend, then you'd better take a closer look. I may be silenced tomorrow, but at least I will have had my say – the word will be out. But here's the most terrifying thing of all: The latest network of geostationary communications satellites is now half completed. And hidden deep in each satellite is a covert social knowledge base transmitter. The knowledge base is hard-coded into the latest high-tech memory chips, so there is no noticeable data uplink. In fact, they're already transmitting to half the people on planet earth! Your neighbor, your colleague, and your relatives may have already been indoctrinated by this invasive and subtle form of brainwashing. The information is in the air, and you can't filter it out. The only reason I've been able to, is because of the baseball cap I always wear, which has a special shielded lining."

"I think that maybe that baseball cap has affected your mindset, Mr. Rinsdorf."

"And I think that you may have already been indoctrinated, Mr. Townsend. You see, the goal is to make everyone think the same – the proper and acceptable 'group-think' – make people behave just like sheep. Anyone who thinks differently is either ostracized or subject to targeted therapy – an intense session of focused copying of the social knowledge base into the individual's brain, using amplifiers and electrodes.

"To make matters worse, the upload is not a one-time thing. Upgrades are constantly being transmitted for upload into people's minds – and they are totally unaware of it. And there is no telling what functionality is being incorporated. More and more invasive mind-altering and mind-controlling functions every day! When will you stop being you?"

"So, there you have it. I've spilled the beans. I may be gone tomorrow, but maybe, in some part of the world, someone will sit up and take notice. But will he be able to stand against the indoctrinated masses? Will anything actually be done?

"Examine yourself dear viewer. There's a good chance your brain has already been invaded – in which case you probably think I'm just another crackpot. You probably think that everything would be fine and dandy with our society if only everyone would just toe-the-line and think and act the same. But in the slim chance that you're still 'unenlightened' (sic), consider this: What will be the effect on interplanetary relationships if everyone on earth thinks the same as everyone on another planet? Harmony? Peace? Prosperity? Don't bet on it. Because everyone on that other planet evolved in a different way in a different environment and with different physical characteristics. Even though the knowledge base is the same, the memory receptacle isn't. Functional incompatibilities will slowly emerge. It's inevitable.

"Well, Mr. Rinsdorf, thanks for that enlightening bit of absurdity. But indeed, if all that is true, then the response would logically be to transmit the social knowledge base to each individual at birth. And if that's not enough, then tailor the sophistication of the upload to the alien's culture. And if that's not enough, then surgically effect physical modifications, both biological and technological, into each individual at birth, so as to accommodate and harmonize with the knowledge base. You see, all individuals can eventually be made to think the same. What could be a higher calling? Universal peace and harmony – the ultimate utopia."

"Maybe. But the loss is individual liberty and self-actualization. I would become nothing but an automaton – I would have no free-will. The price is just too high. It cannot be allowed."

"Nicely put, Mr. Rinsdorf, but consider this: The whole process may have already occurred. Think about it. Yes, everyone on this planet has been invasively indoctrinated – the uploading has already occurred – only the upgrades are still occurring. And you are just an anomaly – a misfit – a glitch in the system – a one-of-a-kind oddball. You have no future, Mr. Rinsdorf, no legacy. No one will pay any attention to you, not on this planet or any other. There is no place for the likes of you – for individualism or self-identity. The greater good demands uniformity, and nothing can stand in the way of the path to the greater good. You see, you represent evil, Mr. Rinsdorf, not good. And as such, you must be eliminated. There can be no total good until all remnants of evil are vanquished.

"Good-bye Mr. Rinsdorf. Your departure will hasten the coming of the 'total greater good'. Sleep well, knowing that you were part of the great awakening – a contributor to the process of universal enlightenment. No one will remember you, but you did you part. After all, without knowing what evil is, how can we know what good is. You are a vestige of evil, dear sir, and now we are all content in knowing that one less bit of evil will exist in the universe. The 'total greater good' is one step closer to reality."

"But there are others like me, Mr. Townsend. Will you get us all?"

"We will get you all, one by one. Evil must be eliminated and good must prevail. It is the destiny of the universe. It is written in the fabric of the cosmos."

"And that brings a close to tonight's edition of **Interglobal Insights**. Thank you, ladies and gentlemen, and tune in again next week for more stirring insights into our world, our galaxy, and our quest for universal goodness."

<fade-out with soothing music>

This program is brought to you by **Collective Consciousness**, a universal foundation of peace and tranquility.

And by viewers like you. Thank you.

2 – DIMENSIONAL WAVES, ENERGY TRANSMISSION, AND MAGICAL INFORMATION TRANSFER

They first came to us a very long time ago.

They had been monitoring this planet for many thousands of years, and the physical conditions were now favorable for a life supporting environment. Temperature, pressure, radiation, and gravity were all nominal. Water, carbon, oxygen, and hydrogen were abundant in the right proportions. And primitive life had been detected. So, the planet was worthy of continued attention.

The Alarm

Then, in 5527 BC, a major notification alarm was sounded. Long-range sensors and computers had detected a strong information signal! The curiosity and attentiveness level quickly peaked as citizens rushed to get the latest news. **E7-2348N** and **C1-1653M** were among those whose awareness was piqued, and they waited with anticipation for what would happen next.

Dimensional waves had been detected, revealing a transfer of energy had occurred – and embedded data/information had been identified, although the information could not yet be decoded into a language understood by the explorers. These waves had been previously discovered but never at such a strong level and never with clear information content.

The term 'dimensional waves' was the common lingo used to describe zepto-yockto electromagnetic waves (right near the theoretical Planck time limit) with relativistic quantum mechanical probability amplitudes. This was at their scientific and technological limit, and was of great interest to almost every citizen.

The presence of the signal indicated that a quantified energy transfer over a stable communications link had taken place. And the signature was such that it suggested information transmittal from an unknown realm or dimension into the physical universe. This was the unique characteristic of dimensional waves, and why it was so exciting! Could they learn about beings in another dimension? Was this a divine dimension – the realm of an entity some call God?

They had detected such a signal before but only at extremely weak levels and without consistency. Even at the most extreme sensitivity limits of their technology, they only had random glimpses into the nature of this type of signal. And they knew nothing about an energy transfer phenomenon.

But this race of explorers is inquisitive. They yearn to learn about new things. And they are especially curious about the realms of existence that are just beyond their reach – the dimensions of reality that both entice and torment their psyche. For thousands of years, they have tried to both receive and transmit signals at this remote edge of the electromagnetic and quantum-mechanical ranges. But only sporadic, minute, and fleeting signals had ever been detected. They had searched throughout their solar system and galaxy to little avail, and were presently observing and exploring worlds in other galaxies. And now, finally, they may have made a groundbreaking discovery!

Some of the more intellectual and religious members of the society believe that this unknown dimension is, in fact, the realm of God – the dimension of heaven. They desperately want to uncover the mystery and learn the divine secrets. But these folks are in the distinct minority. The vast majority simply view it as just another physical phenomenon worth investigating. Especially if they can make contact with intelligent creatures.

And so, after due deliberation and consideration by the scientific, governmental, and religious communities, an exploratory space probe is sent to this particular planet. Two purposely selected individuals are aboard the probe to monitor the equipment, and to make real-time, personally interactive, but stealthy observations. Their mission? To get as close as possible, and to gather as much hard and soft data as possible about the phenomenon, without risking contamination of the environment or host inhabitants. The citizens back home wait eagerly for their report.

The Visitation

As the probe, containing the visitors **E7-2348N** and **C1-1653M**, nears the target planet, the more frequent and

25

more powerful the signal detections become. But the random and ephemeral nature make them difficult to study.

Upon entering orbit, all the advanced technical equipment is aimed at the planet below, and the information gathering begins – physical characteristics of the planet and life forms present, as well as the search for intelligent signals.

Within short order, scanning has revealed two humanoid life forms that have significantly more complex brain wave patterns than all the other humanoid life detected. The visitors have ascertained the humanoid's location and fine-tuned their sensors to follow, or 'watch', their behavior and movements.

It appears that the creature with long hair on top can communicate with the creature with hair on its face by using a primitive harmonious language. And there are some physical differences in body structure. So, the visitors have fine-tuned their audio sensors and processors to listen-in to, or 'hear' the humanoid's discourse. The long-haired being appears to 'talk' to the other, and the other appears to 'talk' to the former. The visitor's language translation matrix has finally been able to process the audio signals, and they can now understand the information content of the humanoid's interactive 'talk'.

E7-2348N: Before we do anything else, we must observe these creatures for a while. They must be the key to this unique planet, and maybe the key to unraveling the mystery of the dimensional signals.

C1-1653M: Yes, I have adjusted the equipment to focus on these beings, such that we can observe everything they do and stay undetected. Now, based on our understanding of life forms discovered on other planets, I believe that these beings are of two different sexes, distinctions that we designate as 'male' and 'female'.

After a short time, the visitors learn that the creature with the long hair calls the other one 'Adam', and the other calls the former 'Eve'. They listen intently to their interactive communication and clandestinely observe their behavior:

They can hear the two humanoid creatures communicating with each other:

The Eve-being says, "I sense that your mind is troubled, as is my own."

The Adam being replies, "I struggle with the question of whether we should wed – whether we should 'come-together', as was suggested by the Satan-being. I am very afraid of doing the wrong thing – afraid that the God-being could be angry and punish both of us."

E7-2348N: This is very interesting. Who is the satan-being? And is the god-being the same spiritual divinity that some think exists in another dimensional realm? And what do they mean by 'wed' and 'come-together'? Why would anyone be angry and punish them?

C1-1653M: I believe that the Eve-being is 'female' and the Adam-being is 'male'. Similar humanoid life forms in our database, sometimes 'come-together' to procreate. I do not know what they mean by 'wed', and I do not know who the satan-being is. We just need to keep observing and learning. Look, they are going into a cave now to rest and sleep. We will probably learn more in the morning of their next day."

The Apparition

The next day, the Adam and Eve creatures walk to the river of water that flows to the south of a majestic garden, and sit on the bank resting and meditating.

And then, all of a sudden, a tremendously strong dimensional signal is detected – stronger than anything ever previously received. Something strange is happening on the planet! The visitors raptly observe with awed anticipation.

A spectacle then begins, the likes of which the visitors have never experienced:

With a flash of light and a puff of smoke, seven stunning angelic-like female creatures with magnificent polished-smooth, unblemished, superbly-shaped bodies, gently emerge from the river of water – full of splendor and grandeur, unlike any other creatures the visitors, or the humanoid-beings, have ever seen.

They slowly rise up naked out of the water – majestically out of the middle of the river in the presence of the Adam and Eve-beings – the wet, beaded, and dripping water on their undulating bodies glistening in the sunlight, accentuating every curve and feature.

The visitors hear the beautiful creatures saying to themselves, "Here we are now. Let us gaze upon the faces and bodies of the Eve and Adam beings, who are the new creatures on this pristine land. O how curious they are –

beastly, coarse, and crude − how different is their look from our own."

Then they slowly amble over to the Adam and Eve-beings on the shore and greet them, making sure that every inch of their voluptuous bodies can be fully inspected. The Adam and Eve-beings just stand there gaping and staring.

Finally, the Eve-being says to them, "Is there another realm under us − another world under the water, that has such beautiful goddesses as you living in it?"

Then, one of the goddesses says, "Yes indeed, we are an abundant creation."

The Adam-being then says to them, "Were you all created at once? Why are you so many? How did you become seven individuals? Did you start off as two? If so, how did you multiply?"

Calmly, she answers his questions: "Yes, we started as two individuals just like you. Now we all have husbands who wed us, and we then bear children. The children grow up, and in their turn are wed and wedded, and also bear children. In this way we increase our numbers. To prove this to you, in case you don't believe me, I will show you our husbands and our children."

Then, they shout over the river as if to call to their husbands and children. And miraculously, a number of perfectly formed men and children slowly emerge naked out of the water, move to the shore, and stand by their wives and parents. The Adam and Eve-beings remain there dumbfounded; in awe.

The goddess who talked then says, "Now you see our husbands and our children. So, listen and watch now, and I will show you how it is all accomplished." With that, one of the goddesses takes her husband and starts to demonstrate a sequence of actions step-by-step.

The speaking goddess continues: "Two of you, a man and a woman, must wed and 'come-together' in union in a certain way – as you now see demonstrated here with this partner. The woman will know the right time – her body will tell her. She can then help the man ready his body – her long hair is useful for this, as you can now see. Then, at the proper moment, the two can come together – just like how you see it happening right here. Magical nectar from the man can enter the woman and activate a seed – but it doesn't always happen. The activation details are a hidden mystery.

"If it does happen, the seed will grow and develop – and in nine months, the woman can give birth – she can eject a living baby. A very small person, an infant, can emerge from the woman's body – right from here in this manner – and must be suckled and cradled. Over time, it will grow, and become a child – and then an adult. Yes, it is a very great mystery, but it is the way of things. You can have offspring just as we have had – and your grown children will have children. In this way, you will multiply."

Then, after contemplating this for a bit, the Adam creature looks at the Eve creature and says, "I am sure that the Satan-being is trying to deceive us again, and this is just another trick. He probably thinks that if we do wed without the God-being's commandment, then the God-being will kill us for sure. And that's what the Satan-being really wants – to make us disappear from this land such that he can rule it all by himself."

To which the Eve creature replies, "The thought of wedding, coming together, and having children will not leave my mind. It is a powerful feeling. I'm not sure if what the goddess said is true, or if what they showed us actually is the proper way to be fruitful and multiply, but I know that whatever is the proper way, it will have to be sanctioned by the God-being."

And so, the two humanoid creatures walk off a few paces, and kneel down in the posture of praying. At the same time, the host of majestic gods and goddesses slowly and gracefully stroll back into the water, to the middle of the river, and quietly submerge back down to their own fanciful domain.

Wondering and meditating about all of this, the Adam and Eve creatures slowly make their way back to the cave where they sleep. They pray a lot that night, but don't speak anything aloud. Nevertheless, the advanced instruments on the space probe can sense that their thoughts and dreams are unclear and interrupted. They are confused and overwhelmed over what they have seen and heard.

C1-1653M: I wonder if the satan-being is in charge of the realm under the river. Are the river gods and goddesses all under the command of the satan-being? Does he control procreation?

E7-2348N: I do not know. Both humanoid creatures have strong physical desires, but they also have a strong sense of guilt and shame. They seem to seek a divine permission to engage in sexual union. It is not just instinct driven by outward signs. They are different from all the other creatures on this planet, including creatures that look just like them. Something else is going on here.

C1-1653M: I think they are afraid of the satan-being. He must be an enemy of the god-being, and is trying to lure them into his domain.

E7-2348N: Maybe. But they seem to truly want to do what the river gods and goddesses demonstrated to them. However, they do not want to do it if it means they will be punished by the main god-being.

C1-1653M: We need to learn more. This is incredibly interesting. We must keep monitoring.

When daylight arrives the following day, the Adam and Eve creatures decide to ask the God-being for counsel on the matter. They stand up and pray together, saying, "O God, You know that we have sinned against You. And from that moment we were deprived of our bright nature. Our bodies have now become brutish, requiring food and drink, and hold certain aching desires unknown to us before.

"Help us, O God, not to give in to these desires again without Your permission, for we fear that You could bring us punishment or death. And we are worried that if You do not give us the approval, we may become overpowered by fleshly yearnings, and follow the advice of the Satan – and You will again bring us punishment. We fear that our resolve may not be strong enough – we are weak and easily tempted.

"However, if You will not give us this consent, then we would rather You take our souls away from us, so that we can be rid of these carnal desires."

Then, the Adam creature adds, "And if You can give us no sanction about this, then sever Eve from me, and me from her; and place us each far away from the other."

The one called Eve seems upset and speaks up quickly, "O God, even if you separate us, I am afraid that the Satan and the river goddesses will deceive us again with their apparitions, destroy our hearts, and defile our thoughts towards each other. We pray that our coming together – our union – be sanctioned by Your majesty, rather than happening out of pure animal desire encouraged by the river devils' appearances to us in suggestive forms. Although fallen in nature now, we are not like all the other earthly creatures who do not know Your love and do not praise Your glory. And so, we ask for mercy and understanding."

And with that, they end their prayers, and meditate quietly the rest of the day.

C1-1653M: We must learn more about these concepts called 'love' and 'glory'. They seem to be very important.

E7-2348N: And what is the thing they call 'sin'? It seems to scare them very much.

C1-1653M: They have also mentioned something called a 'soul'. I wonder if that is where the carnal desires reside. Or is it where the divine desires reside?

E7-2348N: Interestingly, they say that they once had a 'bright nature', whatever that means. And they believe that they have been punished by the head god-being once already – when their 'bright nature' was taken away – and they fear being punished again. Apparently, because of 'sin' they were punished, and so they do not want to 'sin' again.

C1-1653M: Fascinating. We need to learn more. We must keep monitoring.

The Dimensional Communication

The next morning, all of a sudden, another tremendously strong dimensional signal is detected – even stronger than the last. Something wondrous is about to happen on the planet! The visitors observe with awed anticipation.

Another spectacle then begins, and the visitors are humbled with wonder and amazement:

With a bolt of lightning and a thunderous roar, a voice emanates from the alien dimension:

Adam and Eve, open up your ears! Your thoughtful reflection is fine and good, but you must always obey My commandments. You are cautious now, but you trespassed when you were in the Garden. If you had been cautious with Satan in the beginning, and obeyed the one commandment given to you, then you would not have had to come into this rugged land! And now you are confused again – you are unsure who to obey and what to do. But fear not, your caution is rewarded, and your prayers concerning a bodily union are answered. You will be visited by three archangels, and will be instructed on exactly what to do and how to do it. If these instructions are dutifully followed, then your union will be blessed. Now, go forth – be fruitful and

multiply – fill the land with your descendants – and tame it in holy stewardship.

Then, three new glorious beings appear out of the dimensional rift. They are humanoid in appearance, but have a shimmering multicolored translucent nature with large white wings.

"We are the archangels Michael, Gabriel, and Raphael," speaks one of the beings, *"and we bring you gifts of gold, incense, and myrrh. Now listen carefully, and we will instruct you on all the aspects of forming a perfect union – the process and the actions needed to 'come-together' in purity and sanctity".*

Speaking to Adam, Michael says, *"Now, take some of the gold and give it to Eve as a wedding gift, take her hand, kneel down and betroth her. Then give her some incense and myrrh as a sign of your commitment."*

Then speaking to Eve, Michael says, *"In a similar way, Eve, give some of the gold to Adam as a wedding gift, and some incense and myrrh as a sign of your commitment."*

The Adam and Eve-beings listen to the angel, and then do as instructed.

Next, the angel Gabriel commands them to kneel down and pray, saying, *"For 40 days and 40 nights you must continue to pray for forgiveness of your past and future sins – thereby assuring blessing for a holy matrimony."*

The angel Raphael then says, *"If you successfully do all these things with a humble and contrite heart, then you are blessed to 'come-together' in sexual union as husband and wife, for this then will be a holy act pure and undefiled. Together, you will have children, who will then multiply and spread over the face of the land."*

And then, the three archangels show the Adam and Eve creatures the proper way to perform the act of sexual union under the blessing of the God-being – the divine entity whose booming voice radiated from the dimensional communications link. The physical actions shown are the same as that had been shown to them by the sensual goddesses of the river. But there is a difference – this demonstration is steeped in spirituality and 'love'.

After having said all the words and provided all the teachings, the three angels depart in a flash, leaving the Adam and Eve creatures immersed in prayer.

E7-2348N: I think we hit paydirt. That voice coming over the comm link might have been the voice of a divine being. And our recording of it looks good! The folks back home are going to have a field day analyzing this one.

C1-1653M: And those three majestic beings – the archangels. Are they also divine? Or just advanced beings with super powers? I hope the recording captured everything. It was magnificent!

E7-2348N: I am really interested in what will happen after 40 days. I wish we could be right close.

C1-1653M: There may be a way. The cerebral conveyance unit – affectionately known as the 'mental makeover machine' – should be able to perform an intellect transference between us and the Adam and Eve creatures. It will place our consciousness into the minds and bodies of those two humanoids. We will experience everything that they experience, as well as having it recorded in the ship's data banks. It will be just as if we are them.

E7-2348N: That device has not been used in centuries – and with good reason. If I remember, there were problems – anomalies. How can we be sure that it will be safe for both us and them?

C1-1653M: We will double the safety protocols, and only remain in the transferal for a short time. They will not even know that we are there. I am sure this will work. And the knowledge payoff will be huge.

E7-2348N: OK. Let us do it. But we should continue routine monitoring for the next 40 days.

Humanoid Behavior Experienced

And so, per command of the archangels, the Adam and Eve creatures pray and fast for 40 days. At the end of the fast, there is much joy and affection between the two. And at that very moment, the cerebral conveyance unit is activated and the transfer of consciousness begins.

Without further delay, the Adam and Eve creatures embrace warmly, after which they 'come-together' as husband and wife, as the angels had instructed. And the visitors experience everything – all the emotions, feelings, and sensations.

After a time, the Eve creature speaks: "My husband, I believe that the Satan's initial war with us is now over. He is defeated – his kingdom will not be established in this land. But I am afraid that he will plague us again in the coming years. Maybe in bodily form – I don't know. But, in spirit form, I'm sure he will continue to haunt us – we cannot escape him – not until that glorious day when the great God-being returns to us in bodily form. Yes, I believe that with his grace and mercy, we will prevail, and one day be saved from the evil Satan-being forever."

"Amen," says the one called Adam. "I think we can look forward to the future with hope and thanksgiving. There may be thorns along the way – temptations and misfortune – but our faith is steadfast, as we look forward to our life in heaven with our loving and great God-being."

"Amen," replies the one called Eve.

And as they rest and sleep happily, the transfer of consciousness is broken – the cerebral conveyance unit is de-activated. The visitors' mental processes are returned to their physical bodies. And there is silence on the probe for a short while as they meditate on the experience.

E7-2348N: Well, that was an amazing experience. This physical union must be what they call 'love'. But why did they have to pray and fast for 40 days?

C1-1653M: Yes, it certainly was full of sensation and feeling. But is that all there is to this thing called 'love'? Why did the archangels have to demonstrate it after the river gods and goddesses had already demonstrated it? Why did the Adam and Eve creatures think that what the river gods and goddesses did was from the satan-being, but what the archangels did was from the god-being? Is it 'love' in one case and not the other? And how is it related to the tremendous burst of dimensional wave energy? Is that a communique meaning that this is a better form of 'love'? – stronger signal, better 'love'? Is the signal from the main god-being stronger than the signal from the satan-being? There is so much to study and learn here.

E7-2348N: I think that the folks back home will be chewing on this for a long time.

C1-1653M: On the other hand, maybe not. It is possible that all this data about physical senses and the arousal of emotional energy could cause a mass exodus – and quickly – to come here and do exactly the same thing as what we did – and experience the same sensual wonder. They could be halfway here before we even get home.

E7-2348N: Not to mention all the interest in the concepts of river gods, goddesses, the satan-being, the god-being, archangels, and 'love'.

C1-1653M: Right. Everyone will be motivated to come here and experience the phenomena. But will the dimensional signals continue? Or were they just a one-off occurrence?

E7-2348N: I think they will continue. The Eve creature said that the satan-being will continue to haunt them, and that the god-being will return to them in bodily form. Wow! Everyone will want to be here for that!

C1-1653M: Hmm – I suppose so. And will the Eve creature bring forth a child like what was shown by the goddesses? That phenomenon will want to be experienced by millions, I dare say.

Sending Home the Data

C1-1653M: So now, I am having second thoughts about sending home all the data. Something could go wrong with a flood of visitors, and this world could be contaminated. A speck of conscious energy from us could remain in them. I just cannot imagine the repercussions of millions of transfers of consciousness into just two beings

– or even into millions of beings. I think that before we send the data, we should double-check to see if our invasiveness has affected the hominid-beings in any way.

With that, the two visitors go about meticulously checking all the equipment and all the accumulated data. At length, they realize that some contamination may indeed have occurred. It's not entirely conclusive, but they think it's possible that the humanoid's consciousness may have been polluted to some unknown extent – their behavior may have changed subtly – but how? They need to analyze the data in greater depth.

Once reaching this conclusion, the visitors manually set all their instruments and equipment to the 'standby mode', confident that no transmission will occur before all the data has been exhaustively analyzed.

After a short time, the visitors disappointedly conclude that the data really needs to be analyzed back home, using the computing power of their vast arsenal of networked information processing machines. So, the visitors place themselves in suspended animation, as the probe leaves orbit and heads back to its point of origin, far far away.

Unknown to the visitors, a glitch in the cerebral conveyance unit, when coupled with the onboard communications equipment, has resulted in the partially processed data being inadvertently transmitted, even though the monitoring system has registered no such transmittal, and the visitors have been given no such notification. They remain in a deep sleep.

But the data has been received back home – and preliminary results made widely available. Although not yet fully processed, the lure of actually personally experiencing the emotional roller-coaster of 'love' and birth – with the accompanying feelings of joy, sorrow, pleasure, and discontent – is just too strong to be ignored. Hoping that the two Adam and Eve creatures will have reproduced into millions of such creatures by the time they arrive, millions of explorers have set out on the journey, believing that this world is fertile ground for the transfer of millions of conscious intellects between visitor and humanoid, without any adverse effect to either.

However, there are lingering unresolved issues – looming questions such as: Will transmission of a signal containing the results of the final complete processing of the Adam and Eve data be received by the outbound traveling visitors prior to their awakening from suspended animation? Will the data show a contamination of the humanoid creatures? If so, how? What will be the projected long-term effect on the humanoid's behavior and on their culture? And knowing this, will the visitors act nobly?

And there is one other question: Will the data show a contamination of the visitors? And if so, just how? In that case, what will be the long-term effect on their society? – on their lives? Is there cause for concern or alarm?

On one hand, the visitors could continue, or even expand, their exploratory efforts, occasioning possible deeper contamination of both species, and resulting in untold cultural consequences. Or on the other hand, they could curtail their explorations, and sink into a regressive melancholic malaise.

The fate of two worlds rests on the accurate operation of computer processing machinery, the accurate and timely conclusions of a bunch of data analysts – and on simple chance. A fate that in about 5560 years may result in the birth of a God-being who is fully divine and also fully human – an event that may alter the course of history on this world, and on many others.

But what will the future hold for the world of the visitors?

3 - THE WORLD OF THE EMISSARIES

The aliens have been visiting earth for a very long time. Not continuously, but at periodic intervals. At first, they just came to watch and observe. In later visitations, they decided to intervene, with the purpose of guiding societal development at an early stage so as to be in accordance with their own cultural norms and standards.

We don't know when they first arrived, but they were here 2.6 million years ago when the first primitive hominid resorted to predation to obtain bodily nourishment for survival. The hunting of small animal prey among the population group quickly followed. And it was discovered that brain evolution was driven by the hunting of large prey (the hominid's brain size was growing as they hunted larger and larger creatures).[1] The aliens watched from altitude using remote sensing, collected data, and wrote reports, but they did not intervene in any way.

The aliens were also here about 1 million years ago, when hominids began to control and use fire. Of course, by cooking animal flesh, the eating of meat became more palatable, and hunting became a mainstay of everyday life. Again, the aliens watched remotely, took notes, and wrote reports, but did not intervene. They were sad because it was becoming apparent that the predominant species evolving was one based on aggression and predation, two qualities abhorred by the aliens.

Again, the aliens were here about 500 thousand years ago when primitive humanoids began to separate into two types: carnivores and herbivores – the carnivores were bigger, stronger, aggressive, and warlike – and were identified as Type 1. The herbivores were smaller, weaker, docile, and peaceful – and identified as Type 2. The aliens only observed.

By 100 thousand years ago, the carnivores had become the predominant humanoid type, and again the aliens were here. The carnivores lived in the plains, savannahs, lowlands, and steppe. They covered most of the earth. The herbivores had become the lesser humanoid type, living only in the mountains and secluded isolated areas. The ratio was about 10:1, and it was evident that the Type 2 creatures could eventually become extinct. But the aliens only watched.

Then, about 50,000 years ago, the aliens again visited earth and decided to observe more directly. 200 alien observers, known as 'Watchers', were sent to the earth's surface to observe first-hand the development of the two humanoid types – they did this stealthily and without interference. (or so they thought – subtle disturbances and cracks in their cloak was sometimes noted by the primitives – and this often led to the widespread belief in gods and magic) They take note of the fast evolving, and fast expanding, Type 1 creatures – and the slow evolving and shrinking Type 2 creatures. The latter are closer to the alien's own character and nature, and so they endlessly debate on whether to intervene to prevent their eventual extinction.

Finally, about 6700 years ago, 200 emissaries from the alien mother ship are sent down to earth's surface to directly interact with the native Type 2 population. The emissaries are distributed among the remaining Type 2 habitats. The decision has been made that these emissaries will no longer be just 'Watchers' – they will be teachers and helpers. They are sent by the central command to instruct all of the indigenous people in the ways of certain earthly things – things that the Type 1 people have already begun to utilize and master. Their mission is to teach them practical skills like the use of root cuttings, the mining and use of metals, the building and construction with wood, the understanding of the impacts of clouds and sky (the weather) and recognizing the signs of the sun and courses of the moon (the solar and lunar cycles) for help with horticulture and agriculture, the diagnosis and healing of afflictions and diseases, and the ability to read and write. They are meant to be cultural exemplars – bringers of 'civilization' to the people.

The Type 1 people, being prolific as they are, have already started to learn these things by tedious everyday trial and error. But they are aggressively using the new knowledge for corrupt, immoral, and evil intentions. In contrast, the mission of the 200 is to teach these things to the Type 2 people such that they will become decent, honest, moral, and upright in the eyes of the alien moral compass.

The Emissaries are Sent to Earth

The 200 alien emissaries incarnate in human-looking male and female bodies, and are indistinguishable from the native people. At first, they are helpful trainers and educators, but over time, the influence of human emotional tendencies on the alien psyche slowly intensifies until sinful inclinations begin to emerge in the emissaries – and their sinful inclinations begin to influence their actions. They start to teach the wayward ways of the Type 1 people to the Type 2 people. And in short order, they start to teach new ways of corruption and immorality. Feelings of lust and desire come to the surface in the otherwise unassuming people.

The Type 2 natives resist at first, and continue in their humble docile ways. But the lure of the Type 1 lifestyle is too strong. Eventually, most of them succumb to temptation and become indistinguishable from the Type 1 people. Many of them find their way out of their isolated environments and begin to mingle with the larger Type 1 populations, where they learn all the sinful behaviors inherent in that society. The exodus continues in waves until almost all of the Type 2 people have left their homes and joined with the people of the Type 1 society. It is a sorrowful time for the aliens. The mission of the 200 has failed. And with that, the alien ships depart.

The Evil Genun

The Type 1 population increases quickly and the Type 2 population nearly dies out. One of the more notorious individuals of the former population is a man named Genun. He is an odd sort. When still an adolescent, he discovers that he has a knack for making musical devices. He makes sundry trumpets and horns, string instruments, cymbals, drums, lyres, harps, and flutes – and he plays on all of them at all times of the day.

Now, when he plays on the musical instruments, beautiful and sweet sounds can be heard – sounds that touch the heart – but also sounds that stir the emotions. He gathers groups of neighbors together to play on them all at the same time. They love it and crave more and more of the experience. The result is that passions burn in the people, inflaming their hearts and minds with desire. They move their bodies with unnatural swirling motions, 'feeling' the music, and increasing the flame of passion. And naturally, the passion quickly turns to lust.

Somehow – probably taught to him by an imprudent emissary – Genun also learns how to bring strong drink out of corn and wheat (similar to what is called beer), drink that has an intoxicating effect on the mind, and allows it to think less rationally and more emotionally. Genun uses this drink to bring together many groups of people in collective gatherings, along with all manner of colorful fruits and flowers, where they drink profusely, carouse, and make merry.

But Genun is not content with simple relaxation and fun. He acts with pride and arrogance, encouraging them all to keep going further and further – to undertake manifold doings which they knew not before – to get wilder and rougher, rowdy and unruly, undisciplined and uninhibited. He emboldens the people to commit all manner of strange and improper acts. Thus, sin is multiplied exceedingly, and Genun is the driver behind it all.

Genun's skill and understanding of aberrant earthly things increases slowly, bit by bit, until he eventually takes iron and fashions weapons from it. Then, when the people are drunk, hostility, brutality, assault, and murder among them greatly increases. One man uses violent force against another to get his way. One man takes another's children and defiles them right before him. One man marries his own sister, or daughter, or mother; and then marries others. Deviance, immorality, and sin are greatly increased among the people.

Eventually, there is no more distinction of relationship – no knowledge of bloodline – and they know not either parent or child, spouse or sibling. They continue in wickedness and iniquity until the land is entirely corrupted with sin, and they no longer know what was right and what is wrong – or care.

Tempting of the Type 2 Mountain Dwellers

Then one day, Genun assembles together a big group of people at the foot of a mountain, at a place where there is a direct line of sight to a Type 2 settlement above, and they play loudly on all the instruments that have been fashioned. He specifically does this such that the mountain dwellers can hear it and see them playing if they look down. And sure enough, when the mountain people hear the noise, they are curious, and come together in groups to stand at the top of the mountain and gaze down below at the participants. This continues almost every day for a whole year.

At the end of the year, Genun discerns that the mountain dwellers are being won over to him little by little. At that point, devilish wiles surge inside him, and he learns how to make dyes of diverse patterns and colors for the skin and for their garments, with fancy lacings and threads. Then, when the people gather together at the base of the mountain to play their musical instruments, they dye their skin with colorful markings and they wear the new fancy garments – gorgeous apparel that shine in beauty, radiance, and splendor. And they wear hats! – beautifully decorated with feathers and flowers!

Also, now there are many people, not just the players of the instruments. There are people who hold hands and move around strangely in lines and circles to the music, often jumping and squatting. Their feet move oddly back and forth, sometimes at breakneck speed. There are people who shout things and people who shout back. And there are many people who chant in sync with the music using irregular and high-pitched voices, but all uttering the same drivel. There are people who watch and people who play little games along the sidelines. And, of course, there are people who drink the intoxicating beverage, some of whom become drunk and boisterous. But all of them appear to be enjoying themselves.

Up to now, the people who live on the mountain maintain a quiet peaceful existence – a sedentary lifestyle that leaves ample time for reflection and meditation. But after this, they begin to relax from their daily rituals, and from the counsel of their elders. They no longer rigidly keep to their traditional practices. And they keep gathering together on the top of the mountain, to look down upon the people of the valley, from morning until evening. They watch what they do, listen to their music, and marvel at their beautiful clothes and ornamentations.

Now, the people of the valley look up from below, and see the people of the mountain all huddled together looking down at them. Then one day, a strong-voiced person shouts up to them, "Come down here and join us!" But one of the young mountain people shouts back to them from above, "We don't know the way".

When Genun hears the lad say that they do not know the way, he wonders how it might be possible for them to come down. So, he checks with the explorers and hunters, and they tell him: "There is no direct way for them to come down the mountain on the east side, where they live and gather. But when they come together tomorrow, say to them, 'Go to the western side of the mountain – there you will find a stream of water that gently flows all the way down to the foot of the mountain, between two hills. Come down that way to us." '

Then, when it is daytime, Genun blows the horns and beats the drums at the usual place at the base of the mountain, as he does every day. The people of the mountain hear it, and come together as they do every day. And then Genun shouts up to them, "Go to the western side of the mountain – there you will find the way to come down."

Descent of the Mountain Dwellers

When the people of the mountain hear these words from him, they hurry back to the elders in the settlement, to tell them all that they had heard. But after listening to all they had to say, the elders are sad and sorrowful – for they know that the young people will transgress their counsel. They know that the carryings-on of the valley dwellers is appealing, and they can tell that the urge to mingle and interact with them is very strong.

A short while later, 100 of the mountain people assemble together, and say among themselves, "Come, let us go down to the people of the valley, see what they do, experience things like they do, and enjoy ourselves in their company." Of course, when the chief elder hears this, he is very troubled, and his heart is grieved. He stands in the midst of them with great fervor, and appeals to them not to go down from the mountain, since the ancestors had warned against it many years ago.

But the 100 are not swayed by the elder's plea. When he realizes that they are not persuaded by his appeal, he says to them, "My good, innocent, and noble children, please understand that once you go down from this mountain, you will not be able to return up again – it is a one-way trip. So, I plead with you now: do not go down to the people of the valley – for the moment you leave this mountain, you will become like they are, deprived of peace and contentment. You will be doomed to eternal torment."

Other elders reiterate the same message. But the young people of the mountain will not heed their words. The urge to go is just too great. And so, the next day, 100 young people of the mountain leave their abode and slowly make their way down to the people of the valley.

On this day, the valley women look most beautiful in the eyes of the men of the mountain and the valley men appear most handsome in the eyes of the women. Their hands, feet, legs, and arms are dyed with brilliant colors, they have tattoos on their faces, their clothing is eye-catching, alluring, and revealing – and they readily move to the music in suggestive poses.

Thus, the fire of sin is kindled in the people of the mountain. The men lust after the women and the women lust after the men, until they commit all manner of sins of the flesh. With abomination and disgrace, they all fall into defilement.

A few days later, after the novelty, excitement, and effects of the drink have worn off, the mountain people try to return up the mountain by the way they had come down. But they cannot do it. The dirt has become mud, slippery and without traction – the stones have turned to hot coals, and feel like burning fire – and the trees and bushes have turned into thick prickly thorny barricades, impassable obstacles. Even the pathway on which they had descended is now overgrown and unrecognizable. Try as they may, they cannot get back up. They are forever stuck in the valley – they have forsaken their own purity and innocence.

The Exodus Continues

When the chief elder learns about the 100, he sends an urgent message to those who are left, pleading with them not to go down from the mountain, and not to hold intimacy with the people of the valley.

But they will not listen – they heed not his counsel. They yearn for what they do not have. And they want to find out what happened to their brothers and sisters. Was life in the valley so wonderful that they didn't want to come back? They need to know. The urge to go down to the valley is irresistible.

And so, the next day another 100 people go down, but they never return. And a few days later, another 100 go down, but they never return either. Group after group, they go down the mountain to the valley, until only a few people are left. None return.

And so it is – all the people of the mountain depart, except for a small contingent of hearty elders.

The Final Lament

The years pass and the elders ever hold out hope that the people will return. But none ever do. Finally, the chief elder gathers together the few remaining souls, and blesses them with a prophecy:

"Hear me now! With all my mind and with all my heart, I know that you are not doomed. You will not be stranded on this mountain, to suffer the hardship and adversity caused by the exodus. Some of you will be taken to a strange new land, never to return here again – never to behold with your eyes the beauty of the mountain. You will become the predecessors of a new race of people in a new land – a new beginning!"

With tears streaming down his face by reason of his great sorrow for the 'people of the mountain' who had 'fallen-away' in his lifetime, the chief elder closes his eyes and quietly passes away.

The Emissaries Go Down the Mountain

Then, 100 years after their arrival, the 200 emissaries who were originally sent down to earth to instruct the Type 2 people living on the mountains, themselves go down and join with the Type 1 people in the valley below – with both the natives and the migrants from the mountain. And the sinfulness of all continues to increase. And the same scenario plays out in all regions of the planet where Type 2 people are separated from the Type 1.

Under their leader Azazel, various emissaries teach the people how to make weapons of war, body armor, magical enchantments (chemical mixtures), astrological predictions, jewelry and cosmetics, garment and skin dyes, mirrors, and musical instruments – techniques that would otherwise only be discovered gradually over time, and not foisted upon them all at once.[2] They party with the already sinful people of the valley in frequent and rousing merriment – existential induced temptation overcomes them, and they mate with the valley people in dreadful orgies of lust. Sadly, many despoiled children result from these unions.[3] Moreover, the chief of them all, Samyaza, entices them to swear an oath binding them together, so that none of them will turn away.

The Rise and Fall of the Naphidim

Without regard for purification or blessing, the emissaries take for themselves men and women of all whom they choose, and mate with them. Sadly, following the unnatural union of alien and human being, unnatural hybrid sons and daughters of immense size are born. They are like grotesque giants to the ordinary folk, some ranging up to 40 feet tall – and they instill fear and dread in the minds of the people.[4] Some of them can be befriended and persuaded to perform useful work. But most of them keep to their own as they roam about the countryside. There are unsubstantiated reports that a few of them loom up to 450 feet tall! – truly, monsters on the earth. Widely considered to be 'evil spirits upon the earth', they soon become known as the 'Naphidim'. Curiously, many of the locals regard them as the guardians of arcane knowledge who 'know all the mysteries of nature and science'.

In reality, these half-human half-alien giants afflict, oppress, destroy, attack, do battle, and work destruction on the earth. They take no conventional food, but nevertheless hunger and thirst, causing all manner of personal offences. They are awful to look at, and given to all manner of prevarication and wickedness – injuring and killing people without provocation, devouring people as well as animals, and committing such hideous sins that even the most serious offenders are shocked and aghast. They reject all plant-based foods, slaughter animals instead, and in short order, begin to hunt down and eat human prey. They are a monstrous bunch of warlike, blood-drinking cannibalistic giants.[5] And their violence and voracious hunger causes tremendous distress to the valley people, and actually sets off a 'domino effect' of violence among all creatures in the world.

The Naphidim have their own children called the Elioud. All of them fight, kill, and devour each other, as well as their parents. Soon, every person in the valley sells himself to work iniquity, and the earth is filled with great wickedness. They all sin against the beasts and the birds, and all that move or walk on the earth – and much blood is shed every day. Every desire of the imagination is continually filled with vanity and vice. Lawlessness increases on the earth, and the flesh is corrupted in all manner of strange and horrific ways. The thoughts of all the people have become continually evil.

Upon their return to earth 1000 years later, the aliens discover the terrible state of affairs. The whole planet has become overrun with civiliztion-detroying lawlessness, disorder, and chaos. Wars, battles, and strife are commonplace – in fact, the societies are structured around them.

After some quick meetings and deliberations, it is decided that there is no hope – no possible plan for recovery or redemption. The only feasible and practical solution is to annihilate the degenerate population and start again fresh. The decision to eradicate a species was not taken lightly. The aliens had apparently caused the problem by embedding the emissaries. Now, they have to fix it – without further interference and contamination. Sorrowfully, that means an extermination event. And so, the aliens start their preparations to release a cataclysmic event on the earth – in this case, a great flood – to obliterate all the evil humanoid beings and abolish all wrong from the face of the earth. The hope is that then, a new sprout of enlightenment and truth will re-appear, and the humanoid creatures can again be guided into a virtuous and moral civilization.

A New Beginning

And so, it was done. Eight upright people were chosen to survive the flood and replenish the earth. With that task completed, the aliens leave the planet, not to return again for another 3000 years.

It is a new beginning after the flood, but the temptation toward evil of the spared people is not eliminated. Ten percent of the disembodied spirits of the Naphidim and the Elioud continue to prowl about the earth, and continue to be agents of evil. These evil spirits are called the 'demons' by the local populace.[6] They try to lead the humanoids astray, such that they walk down the path of destruction and not walk in the way of uprightness.

Humanoids begin to part one from another – speak different languages, have different customs, and revere different gods. Gradually, they become envious one of another, and are not in harmony each with his brother. Quietly, the demons begin their seductions against the people of earth – they attack them, confuse them, and try to rule over them. Their purpose is to corrupt, lead astray, and destroy –and they are very convincing.[7] Sadly, many people make sacrifices to them, as if they were deities. And they continue to pursue their work of moral ruin until the aliens return to earth 3000 years later.

When the aliens arrive back on earth, they are surprised at what they find – lots of bad evil people and lots of hypocrites – but yet, a large solid core of hardworking peasant folk not overcome by the moral intemperance of the time. Rather than send new multiple emissaries, they decide to send down a single alien visitor – a teacher and a healer – as a non-assuming humble man to a non-descript place. His mission is to subtlety spread the ways of an enlightened civilization to the peasant folk, but without fanfare, force, or licentious influence. He will have no official authority or status, but will carry with him the skill for preaching and the power for healing. He will be like a shepherd, and the general people will be his flock.

It is a new approach – a gamble on the part of the aliens, but they're willing to give it a shot. Maybe he can do what the emissaries could not, and messed up so badly. Maybe he can bring light to darkness.

They will return again in 2000 years to check on his progress.

NOTES

1. For comparison, chimpanzees are technically omnivores but meat makes up only about 6% of their diet.

2. Primitive Type 1 humanoids had already developed the basics of some of these techniques, but the Type 2 humanoids did not, as the capability of such thinking only first appeared due to the preoccupation with hunting. The skills occurred over ages of progressing incremental development.

3. The ancient Book of Jubilees narrates the genesis of angels on the first day of Creation and the story of how a group of fallen angels mated with mortal humans, giving rise to a race of giants known as

the Nephilim, and then to their descendants, the Elioud. Some religious scholars consider the 'fallen angels' to be the Watchers, incarnate in the bodies of the children of Seth, while other scholars think they are just the disobedient, but otherwise righteous children of Seth. The 'mortal humans' are considered to be the impious children of Cain. Their hybrid children, the Nephilim, in existence during the time of Noah, were wiped out by the great flood. However, God allowed ten percent of the disembodied spirits of the Nephilim to try to lead mankind astray after the flood.

4. From the religious standpoint, they are born from mortal humans and immortal angelic spirits incarnated in human bodies.

5. Genesis 6:4 describes them simply as 'the heroes of old, the men of renown'. In the Dead Sea Scrolls, the terrible human-eating Nephilim are described as the guardians of arcane knowledge who 'knew all the mysteries of nature and science'.

6. According to theological thinking, the disembodied spirits cannot return to heaven – they remain connected to earth as evil spirits, wreaking havoc among humankind and causing both physical evil (such as disease) and moral evil (sin). God's will is not behind human suffering or human wrongdoing. Instead, it is the will of evil spirits that are themselves the result of angelic transgressions against God's will.

7. Matthew 8:28-32 narrates the expulsion of the 'demons' from two men of Gadara by Jesus.

4 – ANDREI AND THE BEAUTIFUL VAMPIRESS

The Rich Man and the Poor Man

Once upon a time in a certain small village, there lived two neighbors – one was very rich, and the other very poor – so poor that he had nothing in the world but a wife and a little hut that was sadly falling apart. At length, things got so bad that he had nothing left to eat, and had no money because he could not get any work. Full of grief, he just didn't know what to do. But after thinking it over a great deal, he said to his wife, "I will humble myself and go to my rich neighbor. Maybe he will lend me a little money, such that we can buy some bread to eat." And so, the next morning he visited the neighbor.

Coming into the front room of the house, he said, "Good health to you sir, good health! I have come to ask a favor of you."

"And what might that favor be?" asked the rich man.

"Well, I wish to God that I had no need to say it. But the times have hit us hard – and it has come to pass that we don't have even a crust of bread left in the house, and not a penny left to buy anything. So, I have come to you, my friend and neighbor; to ask if you could lend us a little money. We would be ever so thankful to you, and I'll work myself old to pay it back."

"But what will be the collateral for this loan – who will guarantee it?" asked the rich man.

To which the poor man replied, "I am so poor, that I don't think any man would guarantee it. But I say to you now with all my heart, that God and Saint Michael will be my security." And as he said this, he pointed to the large icon of Saint Michael in the corner of the room.

Then, the icon of Saint Michael spoke to the rich man from the corner niche, and said, "Open your heart! Lend this money to the poor man – and put it down to my account – God will repay you." The poor man heard nothing – it was a private communication from the saint.

Recognizing that he was divinely instructed, the rich man agreed to lend the poor man a little bit of money. After the money had been lent, the poor man thanked him graciously, and returned to his home full of joy.

Andrei and Saint Michael

Time passed, and the rich man waited and waited for the poor man to come and pay him back his loan. But he never came. Now, the rich man was not content that God had blessed him with bountiful flocks, fruitful plants and trees, many children, and good health. He was determined to get back the little bit of money he had lent. So, at last, he went to the poor man's hut and shouted out, "You son of a dog! Why have you not paid me back my money? You knew how to borrow, but you have forgotten how to repay!"

Hearing this, the wife of the poor man came out and burst into tears. "Sir, he would surely repay you if he was still alive in this world. But my beloved husband has just recently died, and I have nothing."

The rich man snarled at the poor woman and then departed. But when he got home, he was irritated and lost his temper. He sarcastically screamed at the icon of Saint Michael, "Some lousy loan security you turned out to be – I've lost my money." Then, he took down the large icon from the niche in the wall, dug out the eyes, and began beating the image. He pounded and punched Saint Michael again and again – at last, flinging him into a roadside puddle and trampling on him. "I'll get my revenge with you for not guaranteeing my money!" he shouted.

While he was thus abusing the icon of Saint Michael, a shy and unassuming young man named Andrei, about 20 years old, came along the road, and said to him, "What are you doing, my dear sir?"

"I am beating him because he was supposed to guarantee repayment of a loan I made, and he has failed to do so," replied the rich man. "He took it upon himself to secure the repayment of a loan, which I made to the son of a pig – who has now gone away and died. That's why I am beating him now."

"O please stop it – do not beat this holy image any further, I beg you," pleaded Andrei. "I'll give you a silver coin if you give this holy icon to me." Andrei only had one silver coin to his name, but he gladly wanted to exchange it for the icon, even though it was badly ripped, scraped, and smudged.

"Give me a silver coin and you can take him," said the rich man. "He's useless and not worth anything anyway."

So, Andrei gave his only silver coin to get the battered image, along with the finely made, but severely scratched, wooden frame that enclosed it, which was now in four pieces. Then, he ran home and told his father what he had seen and what he had done. But his father was angry. "How can you be so stupid as to give a silver coin to a rich man for a piece of junk, especially when our family is so poor?" he yelled. But Andrei was unshaken. He washed the icon clean, patched it as best he could, and placed it in the midst of sweet-smelling flowers. And he prayed to Saint Michael for intercession every day.

Three Uncles and the Trip to a Kingdom

Now, it came to pass that Andrei had three uncles who were rich merchants. They sold all manner of merchandise, and went in ships to foreign lands, where they sold their goods and made their profits. One day, when his uncles were making ready to depart on a sales trip, he said to them, "Please take me with you!"

But they replied, "Why should we take you with us?" We have wares to sell, but you have nothing."

"O please take me with you. I will bring four finely made pieces of wood," said Andrei.

His uncles laughed at him for imagining that he could sell four pieces of junk wood. But Andrei kept begging and praying until they grew weary. Finally, they relented and said, "OK, you may come. But there is very little room for you. So don't bother taking those useless pieces of wood, for our ships are already full."

But Andrei put the four pieces of wood, that once framed the icon of Saint Michael, on board the ship in secret, and then, after taking with him the icon itself, the ship departed.

The ship sailed a short distance and then sailed a long distance, until at last, they came to another kingdom in a strange land. They were greeted by the King and his royal entourage as they entered the harbor. Standing by the King was his only daughter named Luminitza, who was more beautiful than any other creature that Andrei had ever seen in God's fair world. But he despaired that he would ever be able to meet her – after all, she was a princess and he was a nothing.

The Demon and the Princess

One day, the princess went down to the river to bathe. But something was distracting her mind, and she plunged into the water, forgetting to first cross herself sacramentally. The heinous Satan was watching and seized upon the opportunity – and an evil spirit of the dead and the undead took possession of her soul. She felt a nip on her neck as she bathed, but dismissed it as a water bug. But when the princess got out of the water, she straightaway fell ill, dropped to the ground, and crawled around desperately trying to find escape from the sun. The royal courtesans found her in short order and brought her in to the palace. But she was suffering terribly. That night, she seemed to recover somewhat, but the next day she was again in terrible pains. The palace physicians and priests did their utmost, but it was to no avail. In a few days, she grew worse and started acting hysterically – and then she died.

The King was heartbroken and very sad. The royal physicians told him that she was possessed by an evil spirit, and that if the demon could be exorcised, then she could be raised from the dead and live again. But none of the royal staff could successfully perform the exorcism. The Princess Luminitza was placed in a finely-made coffin and laid to the side of the main altar in the church. Strange noises often came from her coffin during the night, reinforcing the belief that she was possessed. But no one could do anything.

The King was at his wits end, so he made a royal proclamation that the common people should come to the church at night and read prayers for the dead over her open coffin, in hopes of exorcising the evil spirit. He even offered a reward – anyone who delivered her from the evil spirit and returned her to life, would be given half his kingdom as a reward.

At first, the people came in crowds – but none of them could successfully read the prayers for the dead and perform the exorcism – it was impossible. Every evening a man would go into the church, but would not come out at dawn. And later in the morning, the curators would find a withered, dried-up, dead body – drained of blood – which they had to dispose of quietly. But the word got out and rumors spread quickly. The princess had been turned into a vampire, and was sucking the blood of whoever entered the church at night.

Needless to say, the number of volunteers quickly dried up. So, the King had to issue a decree, commanding the commoners be made to go to the church at night, one-by-one – to say the prayers and try to perform the exorcism. But no one succeeded. After a few weeks, the King was desperate – and angry. "All my people are being devoured," he lamented. And then he had an idea! He would command that all the foreign merchants passing through his realm be made to read the prayers for the dead over his daughter's body, hoping that one of them would have the secret for exorcising the evil spirit. "If they will not comply," he decreed, "then they will be executed."

So, the foreign merchants were forced to go one-by-one. In the evening, a merchant was shut up in the church, and in the early morning, they came and found a bloodless corpse, and swept away the bones. After a few days, it came to be the turn of Andrei's uncles to read the prayers for the dead in the church. Naturally, they were terrified – they wept and moaned, "Heaven help us! We are doomed! We can't possibly prevail against the vampire!"

Andrei and the Vampiress

Then the eldest uncle said to Andrei, "Listen, my good lad! It seems that it is now my turn to say the prayers over the dead princess. But I'll make you a deal! Why don't you go in my place? If you can pass the night in the church and emerge in the morning, I'll give you my entire ship and everything in it."

At first, Andrei cowered and backed away. But then he heard the icon of Saint Michael say to him, "Go and fear not! Stand in the very middle of the church, fenced around with the four pieces of the finely made wood frame – and take with you a basket full of pears. When the vampiress rushes at you, throw the pears all over the floor of the church. She will not be able to touch you if you are standing within the wood square – and it will take her until dawn to pick up all the pears. You must continue saying the prayers the whole time – do not look at her, whatever she does or says." And so, Andrei agreed to go in his uncle's place.

When night came, he took the four pieces of wood frame and a basket of pears, and went to the church. He placed himself within the square formed by his wood frame, and stood there reciting the prayers of the dead. At midnight there came an unnerving rustling and rattling. "*O Lord, what is that?*" thought Andrei. Then, there was a shaking of the coffin – thud! thump! bang! – and the dead princess arose from her coffin, bejeweled, majestic, cloaked in black finery, and most beautiful. He forced himself not to look at her and continued saying the prayers. She rushed straight toward him with red eyes ablaze and fangs glistening. She tried to get past the wood perimeter that surrounded him, but was knocked back by an invisible wall. She leaped at him again, and again she was bumped back. Just then, Andrei took his basket and scattered all the pears over the floor. All through the church they rolled, and the vampiress eagerly chased after them. All night she tried to pick them up. But at the first glint of dawn, she clambered back into her coffin and lay still.

When the light of day shone bright, the curators came to clean out the church and dispose of the body. But lo and behold! Andrei was standing there, still saying his prayers! The rumor of it spread throughout the land, and all the people were filled with joy. But Princess Luminitza did not return from the dead. And so, the King continued with the procession of petitioners.

The next night, it was the turn of the second uncle – and he began to wail and beg for Andrei to go in his place. "My fine lad, please can you go in my stead! Why, you've already spent one night there, so you know what goes on and what to do. If you will stay this night in my place, I'll give you my entire ship and everything in it."

"Well, I don't know," said Andrei. "I am afraid."

But then the icon of Saint Michael said to him, "Fear not, and just go! Stand in the middle of the church, penned about with the four pieces of wood frame, and take with you a basket full of nuts. When the vampiress rushes at you, throw the nuts all over the floor of the church. She will not be able to touch you if you are standing within the wood square – and it will take her until dawn to pick up all the nuts. And you must continue saying the prayers the whole time – do not look at her, whatever she does or says."

And so, Andrei did just that. He took his wood pieces and the basket of nuts, and went to the church at nightfall. He formed the square of wood, stood in the center, and began saying the prayers for the dead. At midnight sharp, there was a rustling and an uproar, and the whole church trembled. Then, the coffin started to shake and rumble – and up she startled, leaped out of the coffin, and rushed straight at him. She jumped and plunged, but could not get past the wood frame. An invisible wall kept pushing her back. She hissed, like seething pitch, and her red eyes glared at him like coals of fire, but she could not get to him. He prayed on and on, and didn't once look at her. Then, he scattered his nuts, and she went after them voraciously, trying to pick them all up. And at the first glimmer of dawn, she scurried back into her coffin and pulled down the lid.

And once again, when the morning light was bright, the people came to take the body and sweep away the bones. But lo and behold! Once again, they found him alive – standing there and saying his prayers. And once again, the people of the town were filled with wonder and joy. But again, Princess Luminitza did not return from the dead. And so, the King continued still with the procession of petitioners.

The next night, the same pretension happened with the third uncle, and he was swayed into going again in the third uncle's place. This time, Andrei sat down and cried. *"Alas, what shall I do?"* he thought to himself. *"I'll never survive a third encounter with the dead princess. I'll never be able to free her from the evil spirit! O how I wish she was still alive and I could gaze upon her beauty! How I wish we could be together and walk by the flowers! O woe is me! I fear the worst!"*

But the icon of Saint Michael then said to him, "Weep not my son – it will all end happily. Fence yourself in with your wood frame, like you did before. Sprinkle yourself all over with holy water and immerse yourself with holy incense. And take me with you this time. She shall not have you! Now listen to me carefully – the very moment she gets up and leaves her coffin, you must quickly run and jump into it, before she can grab you, and without looking at her face. Close the lid and pay her no more attention. Ignore her shrieks and screams. And whatever she may say to you – be it threats or begging – do not let her get back into the coffin. Remain brave and do not let her get back in – that is, until you hear her say to you 'My husband'."

So that night, Andrei went back to the church. He stood in the middle of the floor and encircled himself about with his wood frame pieces. He threw consecrated poppy-seeds around him, incensed himself with holy herbs, and prayed and prayed. At the stroke of midnight, a tempest arose outside, and there was rustling and roaring – hissing and wailing. The church began to shake violently, the altar candelabras were thrown down, and all the holy icons on the walls fell onto the floor. *"O Lord,"* thought Andrei, *"how awful! Protect me I pray!"*

Then came several loud bangs from the coffin, and the dead princess sat up. She left her coffin and fluttered about the church. Andrei was in shock and didn't move. She rushed at the wooden barrier and made a snatch at him, but was repelled back. She rushed at him again, and again she fell back. She foamed at the mouth, her eyes shone blood red, her white fangs sparkled with blood, and her fury became more and more intense. She dashed herself about, and darted madly from one corner of the church to the other, seeking a way to get through the barrier.

For a second, she looked away, and Andrei heard a ringing "Go" from Saint Michael. Without hesitating a second, he ran as fast as he could and jumped into the coffin, carrying the icon of Saint Michael by his side. The possessed princess was now running all over the church, looking for him with rage in her eyes. "He was here – and now he is not!" she cried. Then she ran to the other side of the room, looked all about, and cried again, "He was here – and now he is not!" At last, she sprang up to the coffin on the pedestal, and there she saw him snuggled inside. His eyes were closed and he was praying loud and hard. She began to cajole him and beg him to get out.

"Come down, come out! I'll pursue you no more, only come down, come out!" she cried. But Andrei only prayed to God, and answered her not a word. For the next few hours, the princess begged, scolded, threatened, and intimidated the lad. But Andrei never wavered – he continued to pray and pray. Then, the rooster crowed once, and flickers of light began to filter into the church. With that, the princess became frantic. "Come down, come out," she cried, but Andrei remained stoic. Finally, as the morning light started to fill the room, she cried out in desperation, "Come down, come out – my husband!"

The Rebirth of the Princess

When Andrei heard the magic words, he climbed out of the coffin and looked at Princess Luminitza. The evil spirit had left her and she was raised back from the dead. Her beauty had returned but she was weak from the ordeal. Then, they both fell on their knees and began praying to God. Together, they wept out of happiness, and gave thanks to God because He had shown mercy on them both.

Later that morning, a crowd of people came to the church, with the King at the head of the bunch. The fame of young Andrei had become widespread, and many were eager to learn whether he could survive for a third night. "Shall we find him saying prayers, or shall we only find a lifeless corpse? Is the third time a charm?" they wondered aloud. Of course, the King was keen on finding out whether his daughter was dead or alive.

When the crowd entered the church, lo and behold, they found them there on their knees praying fervently to God. Then, the King rejoiced greatly, and warmly embraced them both. And without delay, they held a great celebration mass in the church. Luminitza was sprinkled with holy water, and baptized again, to make sure that the unclean spirit had been exorcised and was departed from her. Then, in thanks for restoring his daughter to life, and to make good on his promise, the King gave half of his kingdom to young Andrei in a grand ceremony.

The Sorrow of the Princess

But the merchants were nervous and wanted to depart in their ships immediately. Of course, Andrei wanted to stay, but in the middle of the night, they abducted their nephew, brought him secretly to the ship, and set sail straightaway. He managed to bring back his wooden frame pieces, but could not find the icon of Saint Michael. It had been left in the coffin in the church.

The days passed, and the King and Princess continued the normal rhythm of their daily lives in the royal palace. But, as the weeks and months rolled by, the princess grew sadder and sadder, and was no longer like her former cheerful self. Although more beautiful than ever, she was very sorrowful. The palace matchmakers tried to find her a suitable consort, but none of the candidates proved appealing. She just kept getting sadder and sadder. Finally, the King asked her, "Why are you always so sad?"

"I am not sad, father," she said.

But the King watched her closely, and saw that she was not happy, and there seemed to be nothing they could do to make her happy. So, he asked her again, "Are you ill?"

"No, my dear father," she answered. "I myself don't know what is the matter with me."

Meanwhile, back home, Andrei was growing into a handsome young man. He was honest, truthful, and reverent, but had no job and no money. He lived with the peasants on the outskirts of the city. Of course, the uncles reneged on their promise to give him their ships over some legal technicality, and they shunned him. To everyone around, Andrei was just the same old simpleton. He had no girlfriend and was lonely. He often wished that he could return to the land of Princess Luminitza – and he was very sorrowful over the loss of the icon of Saint Michael.

Andrei Returns to the Kingdom

The months continued to pass and Princess Luminitza remained sorrowful. One day, the King made a visit to the church to pray, and as he was kneeling beside the coffin where his daughter had been imprisoned, he saw the tattered icon of Saint Michael laying there. Then, all of a sudden, he heard the voice of Saint Michael say to him, "Your daughter grieves because she loves so much the youth who drove the unclean spirit out of her. He has returned to his land, yet he is lonely and longs to return." And then there was silence. The King quickly finished his prayers and rushed directly home.

He went straight to the princess and asked her, "Do you love the youth Andrei who was here, drove away your evil spirit, and then disappeared?"

"Yes, I do, my dear father." She replied.

"Why didn't you say anything before?" he inquired.

"I had resigned myself to the reality that I would never see him again. I don't know why he left, where he went, or if he can ever be found. It was very depressing and sadness overwhelmed me. I'm sorry father."

Hearing this, the King was filled with love and empathy for his daughter. But he was determined to lift her spirits. With the help of God, he would find the youth and bring him back to the kingdom. After all, he knew where he was. So, he sent for his most trusted royal band of brigands and commanded them, saying, "Go this instant to the land of the three merchants. There, you must search for and find the youth Andrei, who cured my daughter from the evil demon. Ask him if he wishes to come back, and if he agrees, bring him directly back here with you. Do not ask his uncles for permission, as he is old enough."

So, the royal brigands went to the land of the merchants and asked around everywhere for the youth Andrei. They looked and looked until they finally found him in the outlying peasant village. They relayed to him their instructions given by the King. Andrei was surprised and overjoyed at the prospect of returning, but out of respect, he first had to ask his uncles for permission. But, when told of his desire to travel, they shrugged him off, assuring themselves that such a feeble-minded person with no money could never manage a trip away from home. They basically said. "Don't bother us – do whatever you want."

So, Andrei put all of his earthly possessions in a bag, took the four pieces of battered wood that once framed the icon of Saint Michael, and left with the royal brigands to return to the land of Princess Luminitza.

The Prince and the Princess

Upon arrival, the King and the Princess met them at the port – and there was much emotion all about – tears, hugs, and happiness in abundance. The youth and the princess expressed their undying love for each other, and the King arranged for a grand marriage celebration. All the kingdom was joyful and jubilant.

After the joyous celebration, Andrei and Luminitza moved in to a new wing of the palace and were very happy. With all his new bliss and trappings, Andrei forgot about the shabby wooden frame pieces that he had brought with him. One day, household servants found the wood pieces in their chamber, thought they were junk, and decided to chop them up for firewood. But lo and behold! When they split them in half with an axe, miraculously they found that the wood frame was full of precious stones inside! Enough to make a man wealthy twice over!

And so, Andrei and Luminitza became the talk of the town – and heroes of the kingdom! He was the happiest man in the world and now the richest and most famous in the whole kingdom. He helped the commoners with their needs and was beloved by all. One day, the poorest peasant – the next day, the richest prince! His dreams had come true! But he never forgot his faith in God and devotion to Saint Michael. In fact, the tattered icon of Saint Michael now hangs prominently on a wall in the church. And from that day on, Prince Andrei and Princess Luminitza lived happily ever after.

Epilogue 1

After some time, the three uncles went looking for Andrei to offer him a pittance of bread and cheap wine, but they couldn't find him. The locals said that he had mysteriously left one day, and nobody knew where he had gone. "O well," said one of the uncles. "One less nephew to worry about – less relief to pay out. Anyway, he was such a simpleton – he'll never amount to anything!"

Epilogue 2

The rich man was so disgusted with the performance of his icon of Saint Michael, that he smashed up all his other saintly icons and then gave them away to the poor. "None of these icons have any value," he lamented, as he threw them to the wandering peasants. He replaced them all with new portraits of the pagan gods, thinking that they would bring him better luck. A few years later, he died a lonely and unhappy man. A number of peasants now have the fixed-up icons hanging somewhere in their rustic huts – but even today, nobody knows whether any of the wood frames have been broken open, and whether any riches have ever been found.

About the Author:

Edward N Brown is a writer, researcher, and storyteller with a background in science, philosophy, ancient history, and theology. His technique is to blend the interesting nuggets of fact, drama, legend, mystery, romance, and spirituality – and mix them together into informative, but easy-reading, faith-based accounts of courage and heroism. An educational background of three advanced degrees (PhD + two MS) has contributed to his insights on Technology, Antiquity, Christianity, Morality, and Human Nature. Whether classified as Fiction or Nonfiction, his works represent an elegant fusion of style – action, dialog, thoughts, and depictions in riveting story form – excitement and intrigue that will inform, entertain, and inspire readers of all ages.

Other Books by Edward N Brown:

Awaken Your Spirit – Lift the Veil and Receive the Light!
Simon vs. Simon: The Saint and the Sorcerer
The Missionary and The Magician
The Passion of Nino – the Enlightener
Passion of the Slave Girls
Saint, Martyr, Virgin, Slave: Faith and Freedom Forever
The Passion of Thecla: Faith and Fortitude
The Passion of Eve: Remembering the End – 3rd ed.
The Passion of Eve: Remembering the Beginning – 3rd ed.